DISCARD

Women in Engineering

Major Women in Science

MAJOR WOMEN IN SCIENCE

Women in Engineering

Shaina Indovino

Mason Crest

Mason Crest
450 Parkway Drive, Suite D
Broomall, Pennsylvania 19008
www.masoncrest.com

Printed and bound in the United States of America.

First printing
9 8 7 6 5 4 3 2 1

Series ISBN: 978-1-4222-2923-1
ISBN: 978-1-4222-2926-2
ebook ISBN: 978-1-4222-8895-5

The Library of Congress has cataloged the
        hardcopy format(s) as follows:

        Library of Congress Cataloging-in-Publication Data

Indovino, Shaina Carmel.
  Women in engineering / Shaina Indovino.
      pages cm. -- (Major women in science)
  Audience: Grade 7 to 8.
  Includes bibliographical references and index.
   ISBN 978-1-4222-2926-2 (hardcover) -- ISBN 978-1-4222-2923-1 (series) -- ISBN 978-1-4222-8895-5 (ebook)
  1. Women engineers--Biography--Juvenile literature. 2. Engineering--Vocational guid-ance--Juvenile literature. I. Title.
  TA139.I53 2014
  620.0092'52--dc23
                        2013009822

Produced by Vestal Creative Services.
www.vestalcreative.com

Contents

Introduction

Have you wondered about how the natural world works? Are you curious about how science could help sick people get better? Do you want to learn more about our planet and universe? Are you excited to use technology to learn and share ideas? Do you want to build something new?

Scientists, engineers, and doctors are among the many types of people who think deeply about science and nature, who often have new ideas on how to improve life in our world.

We live in a remarkable time in human history. The level of understanding and rate of progress in science and technology have never been greater. Major advances in these areas include the following:

- Computer scientists and engineers are building mobile and Internet technology to help people access and share information at incredible speeds.
- Biologists and chemists are creating medicines that can target and get rid of harmful cancer cells in the body.
- Engineers are guiding robots on Mars to explore the history of water on that planet.
- Physicists are using math and experiments to estimate the age of the universe to be greater than 13 billion years old.
- Scientists and engineers are building hybrid cars that can be better for our environment.

Scientists are interested in discovering and understanding key principles in nature, including biological, chemical, mathematical, and physical aspects of our world. Scientists observe, measure, and experiment in a systematic way in order to test and improve their understanding. Engineers focus on applying scientific knowledge and math to find creative solutions for technical problems and to develop real products for people to use. There are many types of engineering, including computer, electrical, mechanical, civil, chemical, and biomedical engineering. Some people have also found that studying science or engineering can help them succeed in other professions such as law, business, and medicine.

Both women and men can be successful in science and engineering. This book series highlights women leaders who have made significant contributions across many scientific fields, including chemistry, medicine, anthropology, engineering, and physics. Historically, women have faced barriers to training and building careers in science,

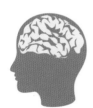

which makes some of these stories even more amazing. While not all barriers have been overcome, our society has made tremendous progress in educating and advancing women in science. Today, there are schools, organizations, and resources to enable women to pursue careers as scientists or engineers at the highest levels of achievement and leadership.

The goals of this series are to help you:

1. Learn about women scientists, engineers, doctors, and inventors who have made a major impact in science and our society
2. Understand different types of science and engineering
3. Explore science and math in school and real life

You can do a lot of things to learn more about science, math, and engineering. Explore topics in books or online, take a class at school, go to science camp, or do experiments at home. More important, talk to a real scientist! Call or e-mail your local college to find students and professors. They would love to meet with you. Ask your doctors about their education and training. Or you can check out these helpful resources:

- *Nova* has very cool videos about science, including profiles on real-life women scientists and engineers: www.pbs.org/wgbh/nova.
- *National Geographic* has excellent photos and stories to inspire people to care about the planet: science.nationalgeographic.com/science.
- Here are examples of online courses for students, of which many are free to use:
  1. Massachusetts Institute of Technology (MIT) OpenCourseWare highlights for high school: http://ocw.mit.edu/high-school
  2. Khan Academy tutorials and courses: www.khanacademy.org.
  3. Stanford University Online, featuring video courses and programs for middle and high school students: online.stanford.edu.

Other skills will become important as you get older. Build strong communication skills, such as asking questions and sharing your ideas in class. Ask for advice or help when needed from your teachers, mentors, tutors, or classmates. Be curious and resilient: learn from your successes and mistakes. The best scientists do.

Learning science and math is one of the most important things that you can do in school. Knowledge and experience in these areas will teach you how to think and how the world works and can provide you with many adventures and paths in life. I hope you will explore science—you could make a difference in this world.

Ann Lee-Karlon, PhD
President
Association for Women in Science
San Francisco, California

What Does It Take to Be an Engineer?

Do you find yourself wondering how something works? Have you ever taken a complex object apart just to see if you could put it back together again? Do you see something that already exists and wonder how you could make it even better? If so, you may already be on your way to becoming an engineer!

Engineers are problem solvers. They like learning everything they can. Many engineers become experts in many fields of science, such as mathematics, chemistry, and physics. They then use this knowledge to help the world. Some engineers work on physical objects, such as machines or bridges. Other engineers are programmers and design software for computers or other devices. Engineers may invent something new or improve something that already exists. Sometimes they are asked to repair a broken object so that it can work again.

Becoming a female engineer can seem challenging. This is because engineers have to have many years of education, and women have not always been able to obtain an equal education. Even when women could become educated, men did not always accept female engineers.

Several very important female engineers have fought for the acceptance of women within the field. Today, anyone can become an engineer as long as she works hard.

Why Be an Engineer?

Engineers are constantly improving the lives of those around them. Many engineers discover their passion at an early age. This is good, because learning to think like an engineer can take a lifetime to master!

No matter what field of engineering you choose to enter, your work will always be needed. As humans rely more and more on technology, even more engineers are necessary. The pay for an engineer isn't bad, either! The starting salary of an engineer with only four years of college experience will be around $50,000 a year. As you prove yourself and gain more promotions, your pay will increase. For engineers, the sky is the limit.

As a female engineering student, find opportunities and support to help you in your education and training. Many colleges and other organizations will offer scholarships to women who are pursuing a degree in the sciences. A scholarship allows a student to go to school for a reduced amount of money, or sometimes for free! If you get good grades throughout high school, you may qualify for these scholarships. Because female engineers are still less common in the working world, others may look to you for insights that they may have missed.

If nothing else makes you want to be an engineer, perhaps the opportunity to see your work in real life may. By being a part of something big, you can say you

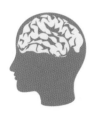

As an engineering student, you may have opportunties to get hands-on experience. Engineers design and maintain all sorts of machines and structures, everything from heating systems to bridges to chemical compounds.

helped create something very important. You could help design a new building or assist in creating a new popular car model.

Finally, being an engineer lets you look at the world differently. You will be more likely to understand why things are the way they are. If you have a thirst for knowledge and understanding, this career will never let you down.

Education

Many people rely on engineers to fix the problems of the world, so it is important that they deliver very high quality work. Engineers often spend many years in school in order to become experts in their field. After school, an engineer may choose to become **licensed** in the specific field where she wants to work.

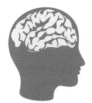

What an engineer does depends on what she specializes in. Engineering has several branches. Chemical engineers make useful products, such as plastics and adhesives, medicines, or even food and beverages. Civil engineers create and improve buildings, bridges, and roadways. Electrical engineers work with electricity and communication systems, including computers. Mechanical engineers work on various machines. These might include vehicles, appliances, weapons, and energy-efficient vehicles. Bioengineers can combine several disciplines of engineering and science to build products such as medical devices or living tissue replacements to solve medical problems.

After earning a bachelor's degree, an engineer may seek a higher education. In total, an engineer can spend anywhere from four to ten years in college. Some engineers choose to earn a master's degree or a PhD. This increased knowledge opens up even more opportunities for them.

After engineers finish school, they must gain experience before working on their own. In order to become licensed as an engineer, an engineer in training must follow a few steps. First, she must pass the Fundamentals of Engineering examination. After that, she will need four years of engineering experience. When she feels she is ready, she will take a second test, known as the Principles and Practices of Engineering. Once an engineer has gained the necessary experience and passed both tests, she's ready to go to work!

Character

Life as an engineer can be exciting but sometimes challenging. In order to do the job well, an engineer needs a lot of patience. Sometimes, an engineer can work very hard without seeing any progress. She can't be discouraged when this happens. A good engineer knows that with enough hard work, teamwork, and research, she will eventually solve the problem.

Many people rely on engineers. For this reason, it is important that engineers make very few mistakes. One error in an engineer's calculations can cause very unsafe conditions. For instance, a bridge could become unstable if an engineer did not account for the weight of the cars that would be traveling over it. A mechanical engineer might cost a company a lot of money if one of the parts in an appliance was found to be faulty.

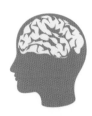

One of the most important qualities of an engineer is the ability to "think outside the box." This is known as innovation. Many engineers invent something that has never been created before. Others figure out easier ways to do something that has been around for a while. Engineers are constantly improving things that already exist. For instance, cars are a lot safer than they used to be. This is due in part to the tireless effort of engineers.

Over the years, women engineers have helped shape our world. The earliest women engineers faced many challenges—but they laid the foundation for girls today to build on.

Words to Know

Licensed: Having official approval to do something.

Find Out More

Engineer Girl
www.engineergirl.org

Hatch, Sybil E. *Changing Our World: True Stories of Women Engineers*. Reston, Vir.: American Society of Civil Engineers, 2006.

Landis, Raymond B. *Studying Engineering: A Road Map to a Rewarding Career*. Los Angeles, Calif.: Discovery, 2007.

Selinger, Carl. *Stuff You Don't Learn in Engineering School: Skills for Success in the Real World*. Piscataway, N.J.: IEEE, 2004.

Society of Women Engineers. "Scholarships." societyofwomenengineers.swe. org/index.php/scholarships#activePanels_

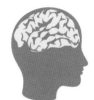

Lillian Gilbreth:
Industrial Engineer

2

Lillian Gilbreth was an **innovator**. In addition to being one of the first female engineers, she was also known for combining two very different areas of study: psychology and industrial engineering. Psychologists look at the human mind and how it interacts with other people. Industrial engineers look at how people are organized. Lillian Gilbreth was very interested in the management of people and how they were affected by being managed. She became known as one of the world's first industrial psychologists.

Lillian was born on May 24, 1878. She was homeschooled until the age of nine, and then, in high school, she became interested in literature and music.

She earned a bachelor's degree in English literature from the University of California at Berkeley.

Lillian began making history in 1900. This is when she became the first female to speak at a commencement ceremony at her college. Without taking a break, she returned to school to pursue a master's degree. She earned that degree in 1902. To celebrate her graduation, she planned a trip to Europe. Before leaving, Lillian went to Boston where she met her future husband, Frank Gilbreth. He sparked her interest in industrial engineering.

Unlike Lillian, Frank did not go to college. His background was in the construction business, and he cared about how people were organized in the workplace. He wanted to find a way to make workers more **efficient** at what they did. Lillian shared his interest, but took it a step further. She recognized that certain things **motivate** workers. These included payment and how they were treated on the job. Together, Lillian and Frank made a great team.

In 1915, Lillian made history again. When she earned a PhD in industrial psychology, she became the first person to earn a degree in this field—and she was female besides! Not many women of her time can say they have done something before a man has. In this sense, Lillian truly was a pioneer. The university that awarded her this degree was Brown University.

The Perfect Team

Some engineers choose to work with a partner or on a team. By having more engineers on the same project, they can give each other feedback and suggestions. If one of them makes a mistake, another engineer may catch it before it is too late. In Frank and Lillian Gilbreth's case, they had each other. Not only did they work together, but they also had twelve children together. Their partnership in both home and work may have been what made them so successful in both places.

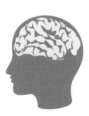

Lillian and Frank Gilbreth with eleven of their children. Two of their children later wrote a book about their growing-up years with their parents, titled *Cheaper by the Dozen.* The book became a bestseller and later was turned into a movie.

When Frank died in 1924, Lillian continued her work. The fact that she was a woman may have influenced her decision to look at how the home was managed. She also made suggestions on how to improve it. Lillian was one of the few people who could say she easily combined home life and work life. She would become well known for this. With her husband's death, Lillian had the chance to show that she was truly an independent woman. After all, she had to raise twelve children alone while still having an academic career!

Lillian became an instructor at Purdue University in 1925. In 1926, she became the second female member of the American Society of Mechanical Engineers. Then, in 1935, she made history once more. Lillian became the first female engineering professor at Purdue. She taught at many others colleges as well, including Newark College of Engineering, Rutgers University, and Massachusetts Institute of Technology. She didn't retire until she was seventy.

When Lillian died in 1972, she was ninety-three. By the time she passed away, she had been given many honors. Some awards and scholarships have also been named after her. The Society of Women Engineers helps female undergraduates follow in Lillian Gilbreth's footsteps by offering a scholarship in her name. There is a permanent collection at the Smithsonian National Museum of American History to honor her and her husband's contribution to the world.

Sometimes, a woman might feel like she must choose one life of another. Should she become a working woman or settle down and have a family? Lillian proves that it is possible to do both. She was an engineer who also had enough time for a life at home with her family. As an engineer, a wife, and a mother, she excelled.

Words to Know

Innovator: A person who creates new ways of doing things, new ideas, and new products.
Efficient: A way of doing something that requires the least use of resources such as time, money, and energy and without waste.
Motivate: Inspire.

Find Out More

Gilbreth, Lillian Moller. *As I Remember: An Autobiography*. Norcross, Ga.: Engineering & Management, 2008.

Gilbreth, Frank B., and Ernestine Gilbreth Carey. *Cheaper by the Dozen*. New York: HarperCollins, 2005.

Des, Jardins Julie. *Lillian Gilbreth: Redefining Domesticity*. Boulder, Col.: Westview, 2013.

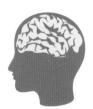

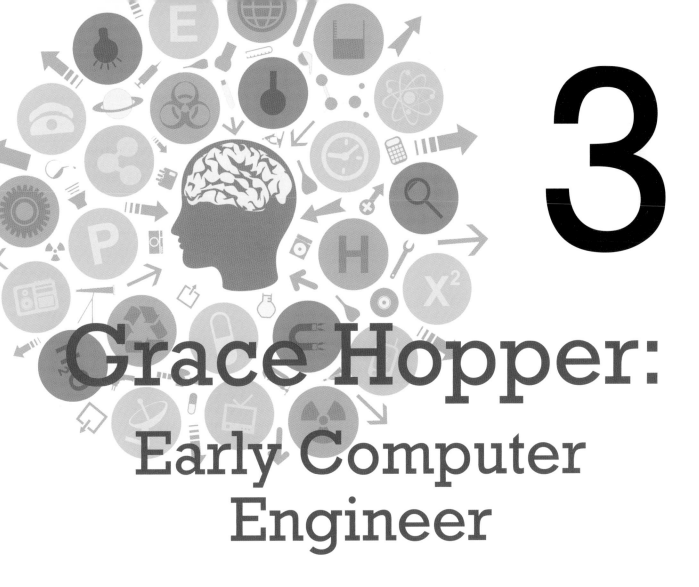

Grace Hopper: Early Computer Engineer

3

Like many successful engineers, Grace Hopper saw what was already there and wondered how she could improve it. It is partially because of her that modern-day computers work as well as they do. However, her life as a female engineer was not without trials. Many people doubted her discoveries at first. It was only after she proved herself that she was finally taken seriously.

Grace Hopper was born on December 9, 1906, in New York City. As a little kid, she already showed signs of one day becoming an engineer. At the age of seven, she wanted to know how her alarm clock worked. So she took it apart. After she couldn't figure out how to put it back together, she took apart several more clocks. Even as a young child, Grace Hopper wanted to understand what made different gadgets tick. This trait followed her throughout her life.

As Grace grew older, she showed that she was not afraid to break free of the **stereotypes** given to females. While in school, she played basketball, field hockey, and water polo. At the age of seventeen, she entered Vassar College, where she studied mathematics and physics. Part of her interest in science may have come from her family. Her mother was interested in mathematics, and her grandfather was an engineer.

After graduating from Vassar College, Grace went on to earn a master's degree in mathematics from Yale University. Then she began teaching at Vassar and eventually earned her PhD, also from Yale. She was the first woman to ever earn a PhD in mathematics from Yale.

Teaching continued to be her passion until the start of World War II. Then, after the attack on Pearl Harbor, Grace Hopper decided she wanted to serve the military. She was thirty-four at the time, and the military would not normally allow someone as old as Grace to join—but she was stubborn. She really wanted to serve her country, and the government realized her knowledge of mathematics could be useful. She finally was admitted into the Navy in 1943, but had to stay within the United States rather than going overseas. This made her part of the Navy Reserve.

She was stationed at Harvard University, where she worked on one of the earliest computer models. Known as the Mark I Computer, it only did very simple calculations. Some of its functions were addition, subtraction, multiplication, and division. Unlike the computers of today, the computers of her time were very large and heavy. The Mark I Computer weighed over 10,000 pounds! Can you imagine having to use a calculator that large? Cell phones can now perform all the functions of the original Mark I—and they can fit in the palm of your hand.

Working with the original Mark I inspired Grace Hopper to create something even better. In 1952, she finished the first ever compiler while working for the Eckert-Mauchly Computer Corporation. A compiler acts as a translator from one computer language to another. It makes the jobs of programmers much easier and gave the computer more uses than simple calculations. At the time, fellow scientists had a hard time believing what Grace had done until they saw it with their own eyes. In addition to creating a compiler, Grace also helped create new computer languages. These included COBOL and FLOW-MATIC.

The invention of the compiler earned Grace Hopper a lot of respect. She was promoted to first director of automatic programming at the company where she worked. Her service to the Navy eventually earned her the rank of Rear Admiral.

She passed away at the age of 85 on January 1, 1992, but Grace is remembered as an innovator and an inspiration for many young scientists, both males and fe-

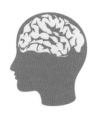

Debugging

Have you ever heard someone say they needed to "debug" their computer? This means they need to remove glitches or fix programs that do not work. The term dates back to the days before Grace Hopper. However, the term was made popular again by Grace in the 1940s. A moth became stuck in the Mark II Computer, and Grace Hopper needed to remove it. She was literally debugging the computer! Today, "debugging" simply means fixing errors in the software.

males. One of her passions later in life was encouraging young engineers to pursue their dreams the way she had. A conference known as the Grace Hopper Celebration of Women in Computing is held each year to celebrate the contributions of women to the field. The computers of today are far more advanced than the ones Grace worked with, but the experts of today still consider her a pioneer in the field.

Words to Know
Stereotypes: Beliefs that everyone in a particular group is the same; an oversimplified idea of what a gender, ethnic group, political group, etc. is like.

Find Out More
Beyer, Kurt. *Grace Hopper and the Invention of the Information Age*. Cambridge, Mass.: MIT, 2012.

Marx, Christy. *Grace Hopper: The First Woman to Program the First Computer in the United States*. New York: Rosen, 2002.

Naval History & Heritage. "Biographies in Naval History: Rear Admiral Grace Murray Hopper, USN."www.history.navy.mil/bios/hopper_grace.htm

4

Corale Brierley: Mining & Microbes

Some engineers aim to invent something new. Others try to improve something that already exists. Corale and her husband did just that. They were interested in gold and how it was gathered.

Gold has been used since ancient times for many uses, including jewelry, pottery, and art. Today, it is used for technology and science. But gold was hard to obtain for a few reasons. First, it was hard to find. It needed to be dug up from underground by miners. Even when gold was found, it was hard to gather. Many natural gold ores have impurities. This means that there have other metals within the ore. Part of a miner's challenge is to remove those impurities. Corale and her husband James found an easier and cleaner way to do this.

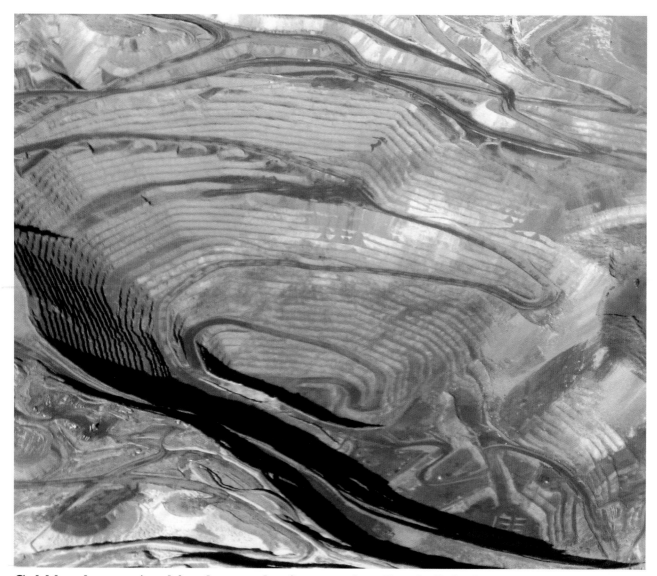

Gold has been mined for thousands of years—but Corale Brierley was one of the first to discover that tiny microorganisms could be used to mine and refine gold more safely.

Corale L. Brierley was born in 1945, and she grew up on a ranch in Montana. This may have been why she grew to appreciate the environment as much as she did. When Corale first started college, she went to Montana State University. It was here that she met her future husband, James A. Brierly. The two would become a team both at work and at home.

Before Corale met James, he had made a very important discovery. While studying **microorganisms** in the Yellowstone State National Park, he discovered

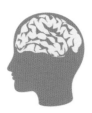

a **microbe** that had never been discovered before. In fact, it was so new that it was named after him.

The microbe James discovered consumed sulfur materials. If he introduced the microbe to an object covered in sulfur, the sulfur would be consumed, while the object would remain. The fact that this microbe existed made scientists wonder if similar ones could be found somewhere else. What if they could find a microbe that consumed all impurities found in gold?

After Corale and James married, they decided to go to the New Mexico Institute of Mining and Technology. Corale finished her bachelor's degree in biology here in 1968. Three years later, in 1971, she completed her master's degree in chemistry. After graduation, she started teaching and conducting research on her own.

Seizing an Opportunity

For scientists like Corale and James Brierley, making a discovery is not enough. They wanted what they learned to reach the world, so they decided to start a company. This is important because it made their research available to the public. It also gave jobs to other scientists and helped change the way mining was conducted throughout the world.

Around the same time, scientists specializing in mining had begun to experiment with new methods to remove the impurities from gold. In the past, harsh chemicals had been used to separate gold from other minerals. These reactions caused fumes that were harmful to people and the environment. By using tiny organisms, such as bacteria, to naturally consume the impurities, scientists could separate the gold from unwanted minerals without causing pollution. The harmful fumes were not created, and the environment was not harmed. This was considered an environmentally friendly revolution in the industry.

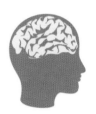

Corale has won many awards for her work, inlcuding the Milton E. Wadsworth Extractive Metallurgy Award.

Corale went on to finish a PhD in environmental studies from the University of Texas at Dallas. At the same time, Corale and James decided to go into business together. The two used their understanding of the effect certain microbes had on minerals to think up new ways to mine. Their company was known as Advanced Mineral Technologies, and it specialized in environmentally friendly ways to separate gold from other minerals. Corale managed the company while James conducted the research and directed the scientists they employed. The work of these two and many other scientists completely changed the industry. Unfortunately, the company failed in 1987. This did not stop the Brierleys, however. They began another company that gives advice and assistance to mining companies throughout the world. It is known as Brierley Consultancy.

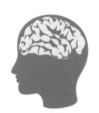

Today, Corale Brierley is admired as not just a **revolutionary** engineer but also as a powerful businesswoman. Women are not common in either field. Corale has also become a **mentor** to other young scientists. She was the 2008 recipient of the American Institute of Mining James Douglas Gold Medal Award for her contributions to science.

Words to Know

Microorganisms: Tiny life forms that cannot be seen with the naked eye.
Microbe: A microorganism causing disease, such as bacteria.
Revolutionary: Causing dramatic change.
Mentor: Someone who acts as an academic, emotional, or spiritual guide for a younger or less experienced person.

Find Out More

Chemical Heritage Foundation. "James A. and Corale L. Brierley." www.chemheritage.org/discover/online-resources/chemistry-in-history/themes/public-and-environmental-health/environmental-chemistry/brierley-and-brierley.aspx

VanCleave, Janice. *Engineering for Every Kid*. New York: Wiley, 2007.

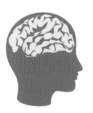

5

Uma Chowdhry:
Beating the Odds

Uma Chowdhry is a woman that decided to beat the odds. Although she is originally from India, where few women were educated when she was young, Uma didn't let that stand in her way. She dreamed of being internationally famous and successful. At the age of twenty, she traveled across the world because she wanted to become a scientist. Through many years of hard work, she achieved this goal. Today, she is well known and respected.

Uma was born in 1947 in what is now Mumbai, India. She describes her childhood as full of laughter and joy. At the time, women of India did not have as many opportunities as men. Obtaining an equal education would be hard, but

Uma works with a colleague at DuPont to develop new products.

Uma was a strong-willed, independent, and rebellious child. She wasn't going to let anything stand in the way of a proper education.

Uma's father thought education was very important. He wanted all of his children to be well educated, even though he had not had a higher education himself. With his encouragement, Uma explored many subjects, but she found math and science to be the areas she liked most. After completing her bachelor's degree in physics at the Indian Institute of Science, Uma knew she needed to continue her education somewhere else. Being a woman in India was difficult, and she knew she would receive a more equal education in the United States.

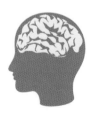

Overcoming the Odds

Being a female scientist in the United States can be hard, but trying to become a female scientist in another country can be even harder. Many women choose to come to the United States for a higher education for this reason. Uma was no different. Sometimes, doing what is best for your future requires making certain sacrifices. For Uma, it meant leaving her life in India behind.

After applying to at least fifteen schools, Uma received an acceptance letter from the California Institute of Technology. Uma describes the day she received this letter as the most exciting day. She was only twenty at the time and had never been outside of India. Coming to the United States would be hard, but Uma knew she needed to do it.

Because she had studied physics and math in India, Uma thought she might become a **physicist**. She changed her mind once she began studying in the United States and was introduced to materials science. Materials science looks at the structure of objects on a molecular level. It asks what objects can do and how we can use them.

After earning her master's degree, Uma decided she wanted a PhD in material science. She and her husband moved to Cambridge so that they could both pursue their degrees. She recalls the doctoral program being a lot of work and very little play.

One of her specialties became working with ceramic materials. Her knowledge of ceramics allowed her to create batteries that would remain stable under severe conditions, such as excess heat or pressure.

A year after earning her PhD in 1976, she began working for DuPont. Her first position at DuPont was as a research scientist. Over the years, she earned many promotions. In 2003, she became the Senior Vice President and Chief Technology Officer.

Uma's greatest passion was applying her understanding of science to the real world. She dreamed of taking the discoveries she made and helping people benefit from them. Working at DuPont allowed Uma to achieve this dream. DuPont is a company famous for the materials it produces. Today, it focuses on sustainability. This ensures that we have enough resources for the future.

Uma and her husband currently live in Wilmington, Delaware. She retired in 2010, but she continues to be an inspiration to many women around the world, especially those in other countries. She proves that it does not matter where you are from. If you are ambitious and dedicated, you can do anything you set your mind to.

Words to Know

Physicist: A scientist who studies matter and energy and their interactions; various branches include the study of light, sound, magnets, electricity, mechanics, and atomic structure.

Find Out More

Chemical Heritage Foundation, "Women in Chemistry: Uma Chowdhry, PhD" www.chemheritage.org/Discover/Online-Resources/Women-in-Chemistry/Uma-Chowdhry.aspx

DuPont
www2.dupont.com/home/en-us/index.html

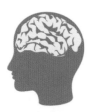

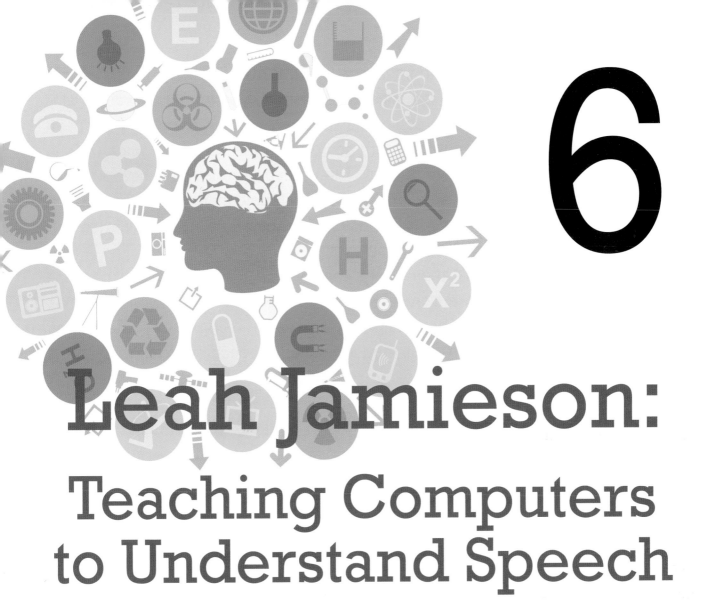

6

Leah Jamieson:
Teaching Computers to Understand Speech

Leah Jamieson is no ordinary engineer. She is interested in two very different areas of study. The first has to do with human speech and how it is interpreted by computers. Leah's second interest has to do with how computers process information and how this has changed over time. She proves to us that it is possible to be an expert in more than just one area of engineering!

Leah Jamieson was born on August 27, 1949. She grew up in New Jersey and went to the Massachusetts Institute of Technology (MIT) for college. Leah graduated with a bachelor's degree in mathematics in 1972. In 1977, she earned her PhD from Princeton University, just five years later. A year before that, she became a professor of engineering at Purdue University and has taught there ever since.

One of Leah's passions is finding ways to make speech recognition systems better at what they do. When speech recognition first came out, it wasn't very accurate. Before a new person could use these programs, he needed to speak sample sentences, so that the program could learn the speaker's voice. This is because we all speak in different ways. The way you pronounce one word may not be the same as the way someone else does. Today, the programs are much easier to use. Speech-recognition technology can be found in many devices including computers, smart phones, and cars.

Leah has said that one of the reasons she enjoys what she studies is because she can talk about it with anyone, even her young daughter! Anyone who has used a computer or a cell phone knows what speech-recognition systems are, even if they might not know what they are called. Speech-recognition systems make life easier and sometimes safer. For instance, you should not drive a car while talking on a cell phone. You should always have both hands on the wheel. By using the speech recognition system within a phone, you can use the phone without actually holding it, looking at it, or pressing any buttons. You can call your mother simply by saying, "Call Mom."

Speech recognition led Leah to her next interest: electrical engineering. Leah was interested in how computers dealt with information. When computers were first made, they could only deal with one problem at a time. Today, computers can deal with many problems at once. This is known as parallel processing. Leah likes to explore how we can make computers better at what they do.

Speech Recognition

Have you ever spoken to your computer or cell phone and watched it type out what you had just said? This is known as speech recognition. It may seem like magic at first, but this process actually requires a lot of programming! For some people, speech recognition is very important. If a person is blind, or has difficulty typing, speaking into a computer may be the only way to have their thoughts recorded.

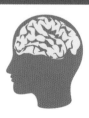

Giving Back

As an engineer, Leah Jamieson feels a drive to help the community. This is why she helped create the design program known as Engineering Projects in Community Service (EPICS). This program invites engineering students to work on projects that help not-for-profit organizations. Many of these organizations do not have a lot of money and cannot afford to pay anyone for the help they need. The students do it for free. In exchange for their hard work, the students are awarded college credit. It also helps the students by giving them real experience that they can use in the future. It helps the organizations by giving them the technical help they need to be successful at what they do. Both the students and the nonprofits gain something, so it is good for everyone involved. Many universities are following in Purdue's footsteps and opening similar programs.

Leah is well known for her service as a professor at Purdue. She enjoys inspiring young minds to get interested in engineering. Her gift to the community does not stop at education, however. She also likes helping student engineers gain the experience they need to be successful. One of the ways she did this was by helping start the EPICS program (see the sidebar).

She has served as the Dean of Engineering at Purdue University and the President and CEO of the Institute of Electrical and Electronics Engineers (IEEE). Leah has also written many papers and received several awards for her work. In 2007, she was given the Women of Vision Award for Social Impact based on her work with the EPICS program. She is recognized not only as a good educator but an amazing role model for women.

Find Out More
Purdue University: School of Electrical and Computer Engineering, "Leah H. Jamieson"
engineering.purdue.edu/~lhj

7

Catherine A. Leslie:

Building a Better World

Catherine A. Leslie has always envisioned helping those less fortunate than her. When she was younger, she joined the Peace Corps as a volunteer. (The Peace Corps is an organization that sends volunteers to other countries to help make the world a better place.) Catherine was stationed in Nepal, a country in Asia. Her main goal while there was to help communities obtain clean water. Sometimes, this meant finding ways to make dirty water clean. Many of the areas she worked in were rural, or not inhabited by many people. Catherine realized the importance of bringing engineering to other countries.

Members of Engineers Without Borders helped a Peruvian village build a system that provided its people with clean drinking-water.

In 1983, Catherine obtained the education necessary to fulfill her dreams. She became licensed as a civil engineer and earned a bachelor's degree at the Michigan Technological University. She proves that you do not need to stay in school forever to make a real impact.

Today, Catherine has more than twenty years of experience helping companies both within the United States and in other countries. She doesn't think the field of engineering should be all about profit. It should be used to help others, too.

Catherine believes that it is not enough to talk about changing the world. You have to find your purpose and go out and live it! Her life is centered around helping others use engineering to change the world. Currently, she has two very important positions. One of them is as a manager at an engineering consulting firm. A consultant is a person who uses her experience to advise others on how to get a project done.

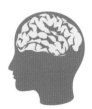

In 2002, Catherine also became involved with Engineers Without Borders. This organization tries to improve the world, a little like the Peace Corps does. The fulfillment Catherine felt working with Engineers Without Borders was the same she had experienced in the Peace Corps. After two years, she rose to the role of executive director in 2004. Her duties now include overseeing the projects being worked on and educating others on how to get them done. According to Catherine Leslie, about half of the students who join Engineers Without Borders are female. Like Catherine, these young engineers are proving that stereotypes about women and science are wrong. Nothing will stand in the way of their desire to help the world.

Although Catherine's job can often be tiring, it is also very rewarding and she would never want to give it up. She's proven that being an engineer can help make the world a better place for everyone!

Engineers Without Borders

One of Catherine's biggest roles is as the Executive Director of Engineers Without Borders. This organization brings the advances of engineering to other countries. Countries that are not yet as advanced as the United States, Canada, and much of Europe are known as developing countries. Many of these countries have trouble finding the natural resources we might take for granted. These include drinking water, food, housing, and energy. This is where Engineers Without Borders comes in. It is a huge organization made up of over 12,000 members with projects in over 45 countries. It uses the knowledge of professionals and students to help people find clean water, build safe homes, and harness energy.

Engineers Without Borders has become very successful. It is stationed in Colorado, but has chapters all around the world. Although it was originally made up of mostly students, it now has a lot of professional help. The amount of people wishing to join the organization continues to grow.

Find Out More

Banerjee, Dillon. *So, You Want to Join the Peace Corps: What to Know Before You Go.*
Berkeley, Calif.: Ten Speed, 2000.

Engineers Without Borders USA.
www.ewb-usa.org

Michigan Tech Magazine. "Engineers Without Borders."
www.admin.mtu.edu/urel/magazine/fall06/borders.html

Peace Corps.
www.peacecorps.gov

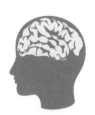

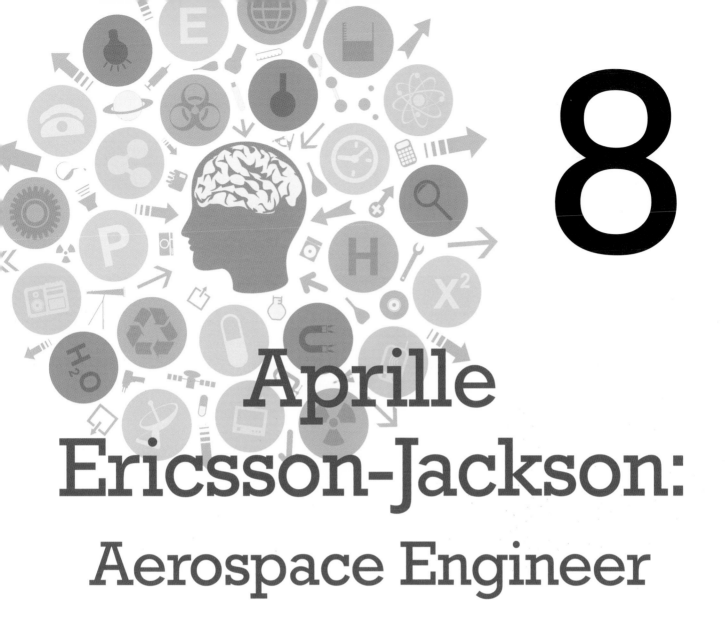

8

Aprille Ericsson-Jackson: Aerospace Engineer

For Aprille Ericsson-Jackson, the sky is the limit. Aprille is one of the few women to work as an aerospace engineer for NASA. Aerospace engineers learn how different forces affect objects in space. Their work is important because it helps astronauts stay safe as they orbit the Earth. Without aerospace engineers, the satellites in space might come too close to each other or even crash.

In addition to being female, Aprille is also an African American from Brooklyn. When she was born on April 1, 1977, not many minority females were becoming successful scientists. Aprille wasn't going to let that stop her. In first grade, she became interested in space when she first saw the United States go to the moon. In junior high school, she became interested in math and science. Although she was successful at school, she was very active in other areas too. Aprille was a member of the school band, the girls' basketball team, and the science club. It wasn't until she went to college that she decided to devote her life to science.

Having Many Interests

Although Aprille is now well known for her work at NASA, she considers it important to have other hobbies. Today, she plays football, basketball, softball, and tennis in her free time. Aprille also enjoys cycling. She has said that she might have been interested in joining the WNBA had it existed when she was younger. By having so many hobbies, Aprille can remain stress free at work. She also says that playing sports helps you become a team player. This is an important skill when working at an organization as large as NASA!

When Aprille was fifteen, she moved to Cambridge, Massachusetts, to live with her grandparents. This is where her love for science truly began to blossom. In her senior year of high school, she decided she wanted to become an engineer. Because she waited so long to make this choice, she had to take physics, chemistry, and pre-calculus all in one year!

After high school, Aprille entered Massachusetts Institute of Technology (MIT). She graduated with a bachelor's degree in aeronautical/astronautical engineering. This degree combined knowledge of both space and air travel. As a student there, she helped with projects that aimed to send astronauts into space. This sparked her own interest in one day becoming an astronaut.

Aprille went on to earn a master's degree and PhD from Howard University in Washington, D.C. She was the first African American female to receive a PhD from

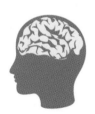

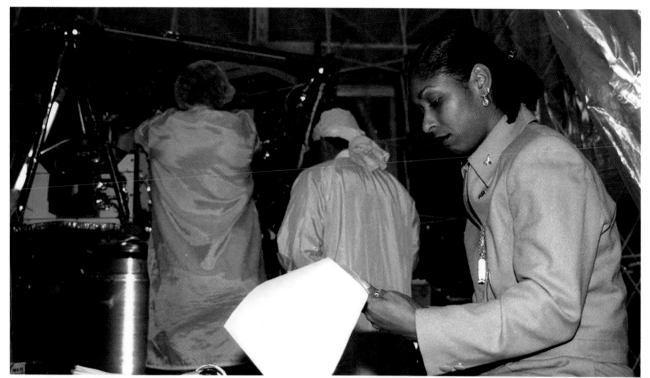

Aprille says: "Throughout the years I thought I might be an artist, a track star, a karate expert, a lawyer, etc. It wasn't until high school did I realize how the pieces fit together. I just loved to figure out how things work and move and I loved putting things together."

Howard University in mechanical engineering. After earning her PhD and several awards for her excellence as an engineer, she went to work for NASA at the Goddard Space Flight Center. There she has worked on many different projects.

Her most important role as a mechanical engineer is to understand how objects move in space. All objects in the universe are affected by different forces. One of these forces is gravity. Another is acceleration. When a spacecraft is thrust into space, it will travel at a certain speed. It must be given the right amount of thrust so that it does not travel too quickly or too slowly. Solar pressure and objects moving inside a space craft will also influence how it moves.

Aprille has helped build satellites that now orbit the Earth. Many of the satellites collect data and observe what is happening on the Earth's surface. There are many different tools aboard these satellites, and she has helped design these too. Aprille's work is important because it helps us understand the planet where we live.

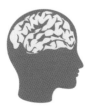

Aprille works hard to inspire other young women to become engineers.

Today, Aprille spends much of her time encouraging young people—and especially women—to get involved in science. As a successful African American woman, she understands the importance of having women minorities in scientific fields. It adds **diversity**, which allows people of different backgrounds to bring new ideas to the table. This is important in a field that is always trying to discover something new.

At the same time, she is also very humble about her own achievements. Aprille knows that her success is not just her own. She owes much of what she has accomplished in life to the people that came before her. Other women engineers and scientists inspired her. For many young women today, Aprille Ericsson-Jackson is one of those inspirational scientists!

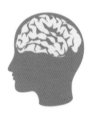

Words to Know

Diversity: The condition of having a range of different things; in social situations, diversity is achieved when people of different ethnicities, genders, ages, and more are allowed to participate in a group.

Find Out More

Library of Congress, "Read, Read, Read—Learn, Learn, Learn"
www.loc.gov/loc/lcib/0104/rocketeer.html

NASA Quest, "Meet Aprille Ericsson, Ph.D."
quest.arc.nasa.gov/space/frontiers/ericsson.html

Science Master. "Space Science: Aerospace Engineer—Goddard Space Flight Center, Aprille Ericsson, Ph.D."
www.sciencemaster.com/space/item/jackson/jackson.php

Sullivan, Otha Richard, and James Haskins. *Black Stars: African American Women Scientists and Inventors*. New York: Wiley, 2001.

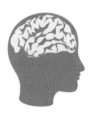

9

Grace Lieblein:
Automobile Engineer

Grace Lieblein is an example of someone who has worked hard to rise from the bottom to the top. As a female engineer working in the automotive industry, she is truly a rarity. Even from a young age, Grace worked hard to prove that working with cars is not just a man's world anymore. Today, she is the Vice President of Global Purchasing and Supply Chain at General Motors (GM), with no plans to slow down.

Getting to where she is now was no easy task, though. It all started when Grace was a student and chose to work for General Motors. Her father had worked at one of their plants, so she decided to follow in his footsteps. At the same time, she was going to school at what is now Kettering University. Grace earned her degree in industrial engineering and then went on to Michigan State University.

During her time at GM, Grace admitted, "Positions like these are difficult for women; but my philosophy is that my credibility depend on my results—and my results will change people's perceptions."

There, she earned a master's degree in management. At the same time, she was still working for GM.

During her time at GM, she slowly climbed the **corporate ladder**. GM has always been a very large and well-known auto company. Today, it owns popular brands such as Chevrolet, Buick, GMC, and Cadillac. Her knowledge as an engineer helped her oversee the production of vehicles such as the Buick Enclave and Chevy Traverse.

She wasn't immune to people doubting her expertise as a female, though. Grace's way of dealing with this was by doing her best to prove them wrong. As an engineer, she was very knowledgeable. When people still didn't respect her after she showed them how much she knew, Grace wouldn't let it get to her. If they weren't going to change their minds, it wasn't her job to make them.

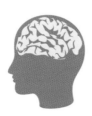

Females in the Auto Industry

In the past, finding a female in the auto industry was rare. Finding one in a true leadership position was even rarer. Today, only about 20 percent of employees in the auto industry are female. This is slowly changing as many auto companies recognize that women can be just as knowledgeable as men. Because half of the people who buy cars are female, a woman's perspective is important. During the production of the Buick Enclave, a space in the floor on the driver's side was created to make it easier for a woman wearing high-heels to drive. Had a female not been working on this project, this feature might not have been added. Auto companies are becoming more open to women in leading roles, but it is up to women to seize the opportunities they see. No one's going to hand them to them!

As Grace's experience grew, so did her opportunities. Like many companies of today, GM has branches in many countries. This is because many of the parts used in cars today are made in other countries. If the car is to be sold in the United States, the parts may then be sent to the United States to be assembled. Two of the countries where Grace had leadership roles were Brazil and Mexico. She was the first woman to lead operations in Mexico. Working for these countries required that she live there.

After being promoted to vice president, Grace chose to move back to the United States. Today, Grace is also on the board of directors for the Honeywell Corporation. This company has interests in many different areas of technology, making Grace's experience as an engineer useful.

One of Grace's passions is encouraging other women to get involved in engineering and the auto industry. She takes time out of her career to mentor young women and steer them in the right direction. Today, there are plenty of programs, such as scholarships, to help women join the auto industry.

Even while having such a busy life, Grace has time for a husband and a daughter. As a female businesswoman, she thinks it is important that young women

know they can be successful in business while still having time for a family. They do not need to sacrifice in either area. Grace is hopeful that other women will follow in her footsteps.

Words to Know

Corporate ladder: The way a person advances in a company or field of work; employees begin on the bottom rung and climb up the ladder with each successive promotion.

Find Out More

CNN, "Can Women Drive the Future of the Car Industry?
edition.cnn.com/2012/12/11/business/grace-lieblein-women-in-motor-industry

General Motors
www.gm.com

Lawson, Helene M. *Ladies on the Lot: Women, Car Sales, and the Pursuit of the American Dream.* Lanham, Md.: Rowman & Littlefield, 2000.

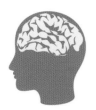

10

Treena Livingston Arinzeh:

Biomedical Engineer

Some engineers receive their inspiration from very personal experiences. Treena Livingston Arinzeh is one of these scientists. When she was in high school, Treena's father had a stroke and became paralyzed. Moving around and performing even simple tasks became very difficult for him. From that point on, Treena became passionate about helping people who were disabled find a way to overcome their difficulties.

Treena became fascinated with stem cell research. This is a very new type of research that is very complex.

What Are Stem Cells?

Cells are the tiny building blocks that make up every organism, including humans. They are so small that they cannot be seen without a microscope. All cells have a special job that they must perform to keep an organism alive. Heart cells are very different from skin cells and muscle cells, for example. Stem cells are cells that have not yet been given a specific job. They can be found within certain areas of the human body, such as in bone marrow, tissue, and blood. Stem cell research tries to find ways to train these cells to replace damaged specialized cells. They may one day be used to grow new body parts that need to be replaced.

In 1992, Treena graduated from Rutgers University with a degree in mechanical engineering. She earned her master's in biomedical engineering from John Hopkins University in 1994, and in 1999, she completed her PhD in **bioengineering** from the University of Pennsylvania. After graduation, she took a position at a company specializing in stem-cell research.

The field of stem-cell research is still relatively new. Despite this, it has a lot of potential, and Treena knows she and her fellow scientists have a lot to learn.

During her research, Treena has made two very important discoveries. The first involves **rejection** of stem cells. Normally, human bodies are very picky about what they will allow in. If your immune system notices a foreign object within your body, it might attack it. This is good when you have a cold or the flu, but not when you are trying to use stem cells to repair a broken body part! By attacking foreign stem cells, your immune system could make you very sick. Treena found a way to introduce adult stem cells to another person without them being rejected. This is a breakthrough because it opens many new opportunities.

Another discovery Treena made involved how stem cells grow. Normally, it is hard for stem cells to grow alone. It's a little like building a house: without a metal framework, the house would be very weak and fragile. Construction workers need to have a skeleton to build around. Stem cells are the same way. Treena discovered

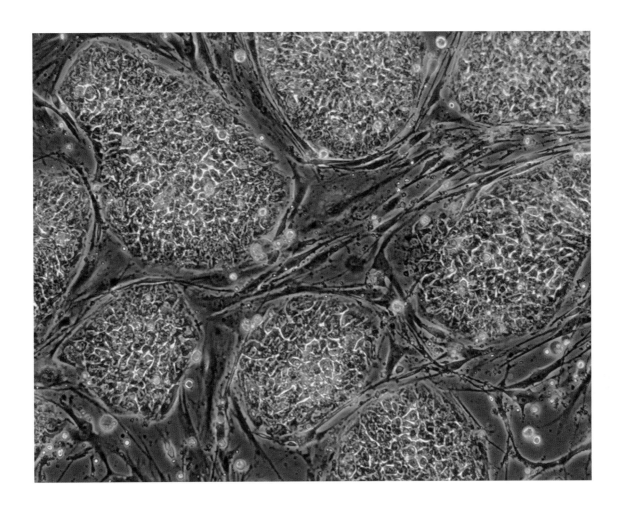

By studying human stem cells, Treena is learning new solutions to human diseases.

that a special substance known as calcium phosphate could be used to encourage stem cells to become specialized cells and continue growing. The calcium phosphate acts like the metal framework of a building. Thanks to Treena, we are one step closer to using stem cell technology to help humankind.

Today, Treena teaches at New Jersey Institute of Technology as an associate professor of biomedical engineering. At the same time, she continues her research in the field of stem-cell research. She has been recognized as a scientist who is always looking for a solution, and she has received many honors for her work. One of these honors was the Presidential Early Career Award for Scientists and Engineers, which she received in 2004.

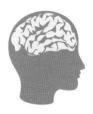

Why Do Some People Disagree with Stem Cell Research?

Although stem cell research can be very helpful to some people, others disagree with it. One of the types of stem cells that are easy to obtain comes from human embryos, or a human egg cell that has recently been fertilized. For the stem cells to be taken from the embryo, it must be killed. Some people believe this is morally wrong because the embryo is technically a growing human baby. Others think it is okay because the embryo has barely grown and the stem cells will be used to help people who are already alive. There are alternative ways to get stem cells. Adults have stem cells in different areas of their body, such as their bone marrow and blood. These stem cells can be harvested without any long-term negative effects on the human that has donated them. Unfortunately, when many people hear "stem-cell research," they still think of the cells taken from an embryo.

In addition to her research, Treena thinks it is important to encourage women and minorities to become engineers. She takes time out of her career to talk with teenagers in high school and junior high about careers in engineering. She's using engineering to make a big difference in the world!

Words to Know

Bioengineering: The application of design and technology to solve problems having to do with living things; some bioengineers focus on plants and animals while others focus on human medical issues.

Rejection: A refusal to accept.

Find Out More

Goldstein, Laurence. *Stem Cells for Dummies*. New York: For Dummies, 2010.

Kids.Net.Au, "Stem Cell"
encyclopedia.kids.net.au/page/st/Stem_cell

New Jersey Institute of Technology, "Treena L Arinzeh"
www.njit.edu/news/experts/arinzeh.php

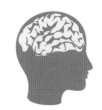

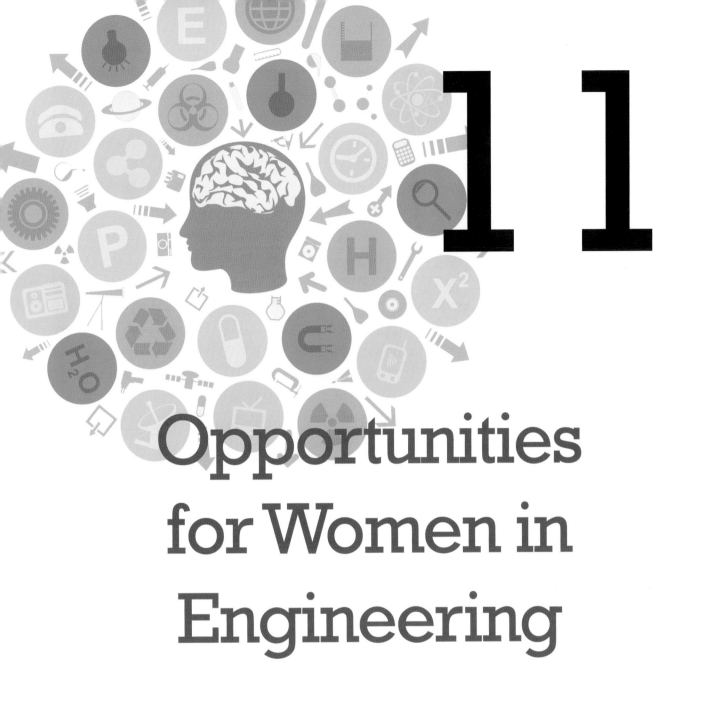

11

Opportunities for Women in Engineering

Female engineers are not as rare as they used to be. Many successful female and male engineers want to encourage younger women to get interested in the field. Nevertheless, the idea that only men are engineers is still a common stereotype. Break free of that mold and think about what you truly enjoy. If it involves engineering, pursue it!

Within the field of engineering, the possibilities are endless. Almost every scientific field has a need for an engineer somewhere, including for research. Many engineers become interested in a certain subject and apply their

Some engineers work in the Army. Maj. Gen. Paul S. Izzo, commanding general of the Research, Development and Engineering Command, congratulated Thelma Manning, an ARDEC chemical engineer, on being the first recipient of the ARDEC Science Fellowship.

knowledge to that field. If an area you are interested in doesn't have an engineering component, you can always try to invent it yourself! Some of the greatest female engineers weren't afraid to introduce something new.

Chemical Engineering

These engineers work on the molecular level. They don't always work directly with chemicals, but they do need a strong background and understanding of them. A lot of chemical engineers work in a lab and use a computer. Chemical

Some chemical engineers work in the petrochemical industry.

engineers find real uses for the discoveries made by chemists. Materials made by chemical engineers have been used in many different products that people use every day. The materials' uses are based on properties such as hardness, strength, and **conductivity**.

Biochemical engineers are interested in the human body and do research in the medical field. Some engineers help invent or improve machines that diagnose and treat patients. Others create new medicines to fight disease. Their

Opportunities in Engineering 59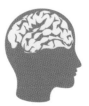

inventions help doctors take better care of people. If you like to help people, this is one way to do it!

Civil Engineering

Have you ever looked at a building and wondered who designed it? Civil engineers work with structures. These include buildings, bridges, and roads. As problem solvers, civil engineers need to figure out how to make these structures safe and effective. If a structure will be built in an area that experiences a lot of earthquakes, for example, it needs to be built so that it won't fall down if one occurs. Very tall buildings must be able to bend so they don't snap in a strong wind. An area that experiences a lot of rain will need buildings that can withstand it.

Civil engineers must understand how the forces in the world interact. Many civil engineers study the environment and the ways it is changing. Civil engineers must also look at society and how it is developing. If a need is discovered for a new structure, it is up to civil engineers to make it possible.

Electrical Engineering

Electrical engineers are experts with anything electrical. These engineers look at ways to improve how energy is managed and how information travels. Today, electrical engineers spend a lot of time working on computers. Computing technology is always improving, so this is a very fast-paced field. Today, there are many female experts in the computing field. If you have a desire to make real differences and solve problems that affect everyone in the world, consider this field!

Mechanical Engineering

Machines need to be powered by something, and mechanical engineers are experts in this science. Some mechanical engineers work with cars, airplanes, boats, or trains. Others work with machines found in an office or factory. Today, most objects are made using machines, so mechanical engineers are always needed.

A mechanical engineer has to pay attention to detail. A slight miscalculation could be a very big problem!

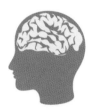

An electrical engineer might work on building new and better electric vehicles.

Engineering in Other Fields

With each new discovery and invention, there is a new opportunity to be had. Some women have invented their own field of engineering just by looking at the world in a different way. These women are well-respected because they can think outside the box. Women have traditionally been trained to be more social than men, and women engineers can use their understanding about society to their advantage. How does engineering affect people and how they interact with their world?

Engineers are problem solvers, and the world is a very complex place with lots of problems. You can help solve some of them!

Words to Know

Conductivity: The ease by which heat or electricity passes through a material.

Find Out More

Baine, Celeste. *Is There an Engineer Inside You?: A Comprehensive Guide to Career Decisions in Engineering*. Eugene, Ore.: Engineering Education Service Center, 2012.

Engineer Your Life
www.engineeryourlife.org

Future Engineers, "Women in Engineering Careers"
www.futureengineers.com/women-in-engineering-careers.html

Layne, Margaret. *Women in Engineering*. Reston, Vir.: ASCE, 2009.

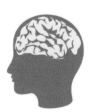

Index

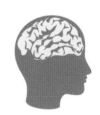

About the Author & Consultant

Shaina Indovino is a writer and illustrator living in Nesconset, New York. She graduated from Binghamton University, where she received degrees in sociology and English. She enjoyed the opportunity to apply both her areas of study to a topic that excites her: women in science. She hopes more young women will follow their calling toward what they truly love, whether it be science related or not.

Ann Lee-Karlon, PhD, is the President of the Association for Women in Science (AWIS) in 2014–2016. AWIS is a national non-profit organization dedicated to advancing women in science, technology, engineering, and mathematics. Dr. Lee-Karlon also serves as Senior Vice President at Genentech, a major biotechnology company focused on discovering and developing medicines for serious diseases such as cancer. Dr. Lee-Karlon holds a BS in Bioengineering from the University of California at Berkeley, an MBA from Stanford University, and a PhD in Bioengineering from the University of California at San Diego, where she was a National Science Foundation Graduate Research Fellow. She completed a postdoctoral fellowship at the University College London as an NSF International Research Fellow. Dr. Lee-Karlon holds several U.S. and international patents in vascular and tissue engineering.

Picture Credits

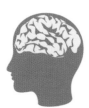